'Zine Scene

by Bobbi JG Weiss & David Cody Weiss

Illustrated by Barry Goldberg

SCHOLASTIC INC.

New York   Toronto   London   Auckland   Sydney
Mexico City   New Delhi   Hong Kong   Buenos Aires

Published by Scholastic Inc.,
90 Old Sherman Turnpike, Danbury, Connecticut 06816.

ISBN 0-439-56287-2

First Scholastic Printing, March 2004

Chapters

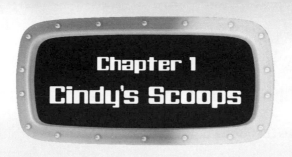

Chapter 1
Cindy's Scoops

Jimmy Neutron walked to school with his friends Carl and Sheen. He was complaining about Cindy Vortex—again.

"I told her it wouldn't work with a regular appliance plug, but *NOOOO!*" Jimmy said. "She had to try it out!"

"So when it didn't work," Jimmy went on, "Cindy laughed at me and said that my inventions *never* work, and that's not true!" He paused. "Well, it is sometimes, but it wasn't then."

"Girls," said Sheen. "Go figure."

Cindy's friend Libby handed Jimmy a paper when he reached the top of the school steps. "Hi, Jimmy-whose-inventions-never-work," she said. "This is the first edition of *Vortex View*. Enjoy!"

"*Vortex View?*" Jimmy said. "What's that?"

"It's a 'zine," replied Cindy Vortex, as
Jimmy and his friends entered the school.
"*Zine* is short for *magazine*."

"I know that," said Jimmy.

Cindy gave a superior grin. "You
might be smart, Jimmy *Nerd*tron, but Libby
and I are ace reporters! We're going to print
the scoop on Retroville kids every week!"

"Scoop?" Jimmy said, skimming the 'zine after Cindy and Libby left. "Oh c'mon, who wants to read stupid stuff about—hey, that's ME!!"

"Wow," said Sheen, "it says here that if Jimmy's hair wasn't so tall, he'd be the shortest kid in the history of Retroville!"

"Wow, you're a statistic!" said Carl with admiration.

Jimmy wasn't listening. "Ooo, I'm gonna get you, Cindy Vortex!" he muttered.

After school, Jimmy
went to his lab. There, he
revealed his plan. "Carl, Sheen—we're going
to make a 'zine of our own!"

"Yeah!" Sheen cheered. "A 'zine just like
Cindy's . . . only different!"

"We're not going to write stupid stuff,"
Jimmy said firmly.

Carl frowned. "We're not?"

"No," said Jimmy. "Our 'zine will be *stimulating! Educational!* Our readers will be *amazed!*"

"Yeah, *amazed!*" Sheen cheered. "Uh . . . amazed about what?"

Jimmy pointed at Carl.

"Well, you can write a health column."

"Hey, yeah!" said Carl. "I'll do inhaler reviews and write about foods that cause gas. That might make the lunch room a lot more comfortable, you know?"

"And I'll write a comic book review column!" said Sheen. "After all, comics aren't just lines on paper—they're lines on paper *with color!*"

"And I'll blow Cindy out of the water with a cutting-edge column covering the latest technologies!" said Jimmy. "Come on, you guys, let's blast!"

It wasn't long before the first edition of Jimmy's 'zine was ready. He used his rocket to pass out copies all over town.

"Ha!" he crowed in triumph. "Let's see Cindy's 'zine compete with *Neutron News!*"

Jimmy hurried to school the next morning, sure he would find all the kids reading his 'zine. But when he got there . . .

24

"They're reading *Vortex View!*" he cried.
"But . . . but *Neutron News* has everything!
It's informational, educational—"

"And look," said Sheen in delight. "It's got a whole column devoted to Ultra Lord!"

Jimmy sighed. "I know, Sheen. *You* wrote it."

"Get with the program, *Gootron*," Cindy said smugly. "We already spend all day in school, remember? Kids don't want more education. They want gossip!"

"Maybe she's right, Jimmy," said Carl. "I mean, maybe we need to do that scoop thing, you know, like she does."

Jimmy wasn't listening. "Think!" he was muttering to himself. "Think!"

"*BRAIN BLAST!*" Jimmy suddenly cried. "Come on, Carl! Come on, Sheen! I've got the answer!"

Chapter 4
The Super
Scooper Scope

Later at Jimmy's lab, Carl and Sheen
saw Jimmy's latest invention. "Behold the
Super Scooper Scope!" cried Jimmy.

"Cool!" said Sheen. "So . . . what does it do?"

"We need to get the scoop on kids at school faster than Cindy, right?" said Jimmy. "Well, the Scooper Scope will detect newsworthy events at superspeed and record them for us!"

"Best of all," continued Jimmy, "using advanced WiFi technology, the Scooper Scope will wirelessly download reports directly to the LCD pixel substrate of this special paper I've invented!"

"Huh?" said Carl and Sheen at the same time.

Jimmy sighed. "The stories will change automatically right on the page as they happen."

"Oh," said Carl. "Cool!" said Sheen. Jimmy just shook his head. "Sometimes it's hard being a genius," he muttered.

Chapter 5
Too Many Scoops

The next day at school, Jimmy savored his victory. Everybody was reading *Neutron News!*

"Okay, Neutron, how are you scooping my scoops?" Cindy demanded. "You've got stuff *in print* that Libby and I only *heard* about just *now!*"

Libby held up the front page. "And a minute ago the headline was about Miss Fowl's new chalkboard," she said. "Now it's about *us!*"

Cindy glared at Jimmy. "How'd you do that?"

Jimmy smiled smugly. This was going better than he could have hoped! "I guess I'm just smarter than you, Cindy," he said and sauntered away.

But later that day, Nick shoved a copy of *Neutron News* under Jimmy's nose. "Was it your idea to tell the world I wear Fuzzy Bunny boxers, Neutron? You're messin' with the wrong kid!" Nick threatened.

Then Cindy stomped up to him, waving the offending publication. *"YOU'RE IN FOR IT NOW, NEUTRON!"* she shrieked.

And then Carl blundered over wearing a bag on his head. "I'm too embarrassed to show my face," he told Jimmy.

Jimmy read the headline and gulped. "Oh, um . . . sorry about that, Carl."

Jimmy knew his 'zine had definitely gone too far when Sheen crawled to him, waving a copy of *Neutron News* bearing the headline: ULTRA LORD JUST A DUMB DOLL!

"Make it stop, Jimmy!" Sheen gasped. "Can't take it—too horrible—!"

"Sheen's right, Jimmy," said Cindy. "You're not reporting news—you're invading our personal lives!"

Everyone shouted their agreement.

Jimmy backed away from the angry crowd. "Hey, I've just got an ace reporter who's a little overzealous, that's all!" he told everybody.

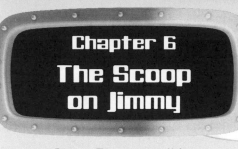

Chapter 6
The Scoop
on Jimmy

Cindy stared at Jimmy. "Ace
reporter?" she asked.

Jimmy pointed up. "It's my Super Scooper Scope. I invented it to do all my reporting, but I guess it's snooping a little too much."

"Then turn it off!" Cindy demanded.

For once, Jimmy agreed with Cindy. So he took out his control device and—with a sigh—pushed the OFF button.

Nothing happened. "Jumpin' Jupiter, it's not responding!" Jimmy shouted. "It was supposed to shut down!"

"Hey, look!" said Carl, holding up his copy of *Neutron News*.

Jimmy read the new headline. "What?" he cried. "That's not true!"

The headline instantly changed to read:
NEUTRON DENIES IT!

"Okay, you!" Jimmy yelled at his invention.
"Stop right now!"

Instead, the headline changed again.

MAKE ME! it read. Then the Super Scooper

Scope flew away.

Jimmy faced the crowd. "Don't worry, guys," he told them. "I have a plan!"

Chapter 7
The Big Scoop

The next morning, according to Jimmy's instructions, everybody gathered in the school playground.

"Jimmy's announcing some new invention," Sheen explained to the crowd.

"Well, whatever it is, it had better get rid of that Super Scooper Scope!" said Cindy. "It's reporting everything we do—

even now!"

Finally, Jimmy stepped up to the podium. "Greetings, everyone!" he said. "I'm here to announce the completion of my latest creation— the Neutron Got Box!"

"Got Box?" Cindy repeated, confused. "What does it do?"

"Watch and see!" said Jimmy.

"Okay, Got Box," said Jimmy.
"GO GET IT!"

As everybody watched, the Got
Box flew after the Super Scooper Scope . . .

. . . and, in one mighty chomp, ATE it!

"The Got Box got it!" the crowd cheered.

"And look!" said Carl, pointing to *Neutron News* in Cindy's hands. The headline now read: HELP! HELP! IT'S GOING TO EAT M—!

Everyone congratulated Jimmy on his
success. "I have to admit, Neutron, that was
pretty good," said Cindy.

"It was awesome!" said Sheen.

"Thanks," Jimmy said. "All in a day's work!"

Later that day, Cindy and Libby gave out a new edition of Vortex View. NEUTRON FIXES STUPID MISTAKE! blared the headline.

"I should have known," Jimmy said, shaking his head as he, Carl, and Sheen headed out the door.

"So, Jimmy," said Sheen, "whatever happened to your . . . uh . . . Stupor Pooper Scoop . . . thing?"

"It's deactivated," Jimmy replied confidently.

"Uh, Jimmy?" Carl picked up a paper off the ground. "Are you sure about that?"

NEUTRON NEWS

PERSECUTED INVENTION PLOTS REVENGE AGAINST JIMMY NEUTRON